Made in the USA
Las Vegas, NV
15 August 2021

28239100R00069